GANG OF DECEIVERS

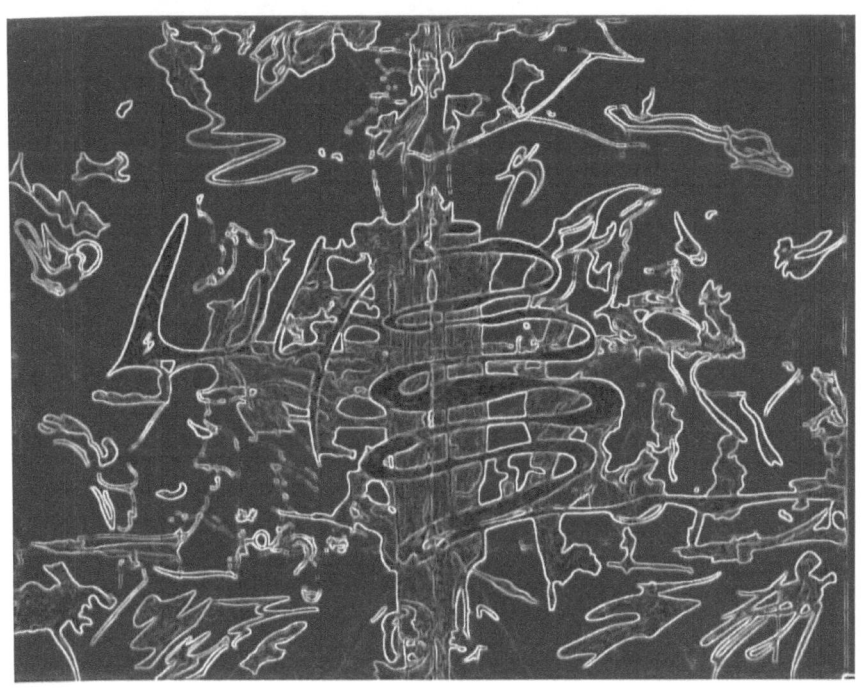

Leo Sayno Demiheyzeus

Gang Of Deceivers

Written by *Leo Sayno Demiheyzeus*

Table of Contents

Chapter 1: The Recruit

Imagine a world where G.O.D. was the ruler. They don't make laws; they don't pass judgment. They execute any actions needed to protect the land. The most ruthless and lawless are given the power to kill. Their influence is exponential. Most people wanted them eliminated because there were some unexplainable deaths. I personally don't care. As long as they don't get in my way they won't be my target. They don't have a hierarchy, but they have a leader. His name is Grim and he just recruited me to become one of his many enforcers. I went with him because I knew he meant business.

When we reached our location Grim gave a proper introduction, "You meet me at the end of your life after you take your last breath. Your spirit greets me. The body, which was once yours, no longer belongs to you. I am the peacemaker, the angel of death. I am the guardian of the *Gates of Judgment*. I am Grim the Healer." He wasn't by himself.

Some guy with blue lips began to speak, "You fear me. You have done unspeakable things. I do not pass judgment. I am an obedient soldier put here to destroy the evil that possesses a creature. I am the commander. I am Ace the Joker." It wasn't over yet. The Joker had more to say, "For now, we are who you answer to. Soon you will be tested, evaluated and given a title. This title is not based on rank. Think of it as a nickname. Because there is no hierarchy you will be given tasks. You are expected to complete them or face the consequences; whether they are good or bad. Now go into the other room and we will come get you shortly." Guess that's my cue to leave. I wonder…

Grim was just as curious as I was. So he asked, "How do you feel about having a partner Ace?"

"You want to know how I feel about having a partner," Ace felt insulted, "Honestly, I want to send him in for judgment."

"Hahaha, that's why you are the Joker," Grim was laughing like a tickled child. I could hear him in the other room. Ace gave a look of disgust. "No need for the sour face you already look like a sad clown."

"And they call me the Joker. Look, I will do my best to train him. What is his importance in our mission? Who is he?" Ace was becoming impatient with Grim.

"He is nobody. He is just another pawn on the chess board," Grim couldn't have been more sarcastic.

"We need true believers. Most of your forces only believe in killing. This is about revealing the real evil. People are dying to live. When they finally begin to live they live to die. Without life there can't be death. Without death there can't be life. We are tolerant and merciful. They should call you God. You answer the people's prayers. You are all-seeing. They call you Satan, the devil; one who is deceitful. They can't even begin to understand. Tell me what makes him so special? Tell me why I am more concerned then you?" The Joker doesn't joke much. You could feel his anger and frustration as he spoke to Grim. Grim has a sick sense of humor and it aggravates Ace.

Grim was still mocking Ace, "Hahaha, stop it. I can't breathe. You're too good, pretending to care."

"Seriously," Ace did his best to maintain his composure.

"Ok, no need to get emotional, as if you could care you cold-hearted bastard. I feel how I want and I do what I want. I put in the work." Grim said with authority.

"The recruit?" Ace asked with no concern.

Grim attempted to lighten the mood, "He is my son."

"Hahaha, now you mock me and G.O.D.," Ace said sarcastically.

"Ok. He is a blind believer; completely loyal. I found him hurting on the inside and out. He needed to belong. He will do anything that is required no questions asked. He reminds me of you, passionate, concerned, and impatient amongst other things. I was hoping you could get him to open up more. It'll teach you something you never knew about yourself." Grim couldn't have been more serious.

Ace was still in disbelief, "Are you ever going to claim the name joker?"

"No jokes, you will find out. And why would I ever claim to be the Joker? I don't make you laugh and I don't look like my sister did my makeup either. Here is the test. This time you will monitor, evaluate, and give him a title." Ace hesitated to leave; almost in a catatonic state. He was still in disbelief. Ultimately, he made his move.

I was in the other room having second thoughts. A fear had invaded my mind, "I don't belong here. I don't belong anywhere. I roam the land taking what I need; helping when I can. I need to stop talking to myself." I sighed feeling weak and vulnerable, "this is my next investigation. Who is my main target? Who cares, I just hope I don't go berserk ever again."

"Come on I can't wait until D-Day." He casually glanced at his board, "This test requires you to meditate. After you finish I will tell you the reason for it and the results. Be prepared to take many more tests. Good luck and I will be waiting for you to finish."

I asked him, "How will I know when I'm finished?"

"You will know," Ace replied.

I asked him another question, "How many tests do I have to take?"

He replied, "Focus on this test. Considering you are still a recruit, it shouldn't matter."

Then I asked him another question, "Aren't you worried I could leak information or use it to take down the organization?" he was getting irritated with me but I continued, "Because somebody will if there hasn't been an attempt already. Oh and one more thing" Ace was about to pop a blood vessel, but he patiently waited for me to finish, "Grim told me to tell you all of this."

"Hahaha, now you are the joker."

"Yeah and you are number one on his list." Once I said that he decided to open his ears.

"Who are you again?" that was an attempt to intimidate me. He said I would fear him, but the only thing that was scary was his makeup.

He finally took interest with me so I gave him a proper introduction, "I am the one you thought you knew. You won't fear me, but you will respect me. You won't understand me, but you will believe in me. I am the unpredictable. I am true to myself. I am Anon the Unknown."

"So you came up with that name all by yourself?" is what he asked in a condescending voice.

I didn't want to break character, but I had to let him know, "I am your partner. Our mission is to *Trap the Rat*."

He began drawing a conclusion, "I guess Grim told you to tell me all of this as well? If that's true then he gave you that name. If that's true then this was a test for me. If that's true…"

"He suspected you as his enemy and now we must 'Trap the Rat' for Judgment Day." I had to cut him off. It was taking him to long to get to the point.

Chapter 2: Unveiling the Unknown

I felt uneasy about being a part of this. Thankfully my first test is meditation. Ace left to go talk to Grim. I guess he bought my act.

"I can't believe Grim set me up like this. He is really testing me today," Ace was steaming so he confronted Grim about his meeting with me, "What did you tell Anon when you brought him here? And why are you still testing me? I've been loyal since day one."

Grim didn't feel threatened. He knew of Anon's habits. So he took a deep breath, and spoke to Ace, "I know that is why you are in control of his fate. Whatever he told you may not be true."

So Ace asked Grim, "So nobody is trying to infiltrate our organization, and you didn't give him a title?"

"Someone is trying to infiltrate, yes. This is why I paired him with you. Anybody else would have gone along with whatever he said. And no, that was your task."

"Ok, so I'm going to act like this didn't happen."

"That would be wise."

Ace went back and saw me meditating so he waited a while until I was done. Meanwhile, I was starting to understand why I was here. Everything I fought for was only part of my resolution. I realized I have the resources. I realized that no matter the choice there are consequences. I can pack up and roam, or stay and enjoy the ride.

"WOW!!!" I opened my eyes gasping for air.

"So what did you see?"

"I saw everything; fear temptation, intimidation, manipulation... I saw memories I repressed and I saw things I've never seen before; I felt things I've never felt before."

"You know why, but do you understand why?"

"Did you understand what you saw and how you felt when you took the test?"

"None of your business."

All of a sudden I started thinking of my meeting with Grim. He spoke to me after I finished running in an attempt to escape my beaten opponent, "I see you are good at protecting others."

I responded, "I only protect myself." He was a stranger to me. For all I knew he was trying to kill me too.

"That might be so, but we both know that is not the only reason. I noticed you have a dark-side, would you mind sharing that story with me? I might be able to help." I guess that was his way of reaching out to me.

"I don't know what you are talking about."

"You don't like to be confronted and when provoked you experience blackout moments of blind rage. I can't teach you how to control it, that is up to you. I will provide a mentor who wants a partner. It is your choice. Hop in or keep fighting against yourself."

Ace is frantically trying to get my attention, "Hello, are you there?"

I was lost in thought but I came to life. "You looked like you seen a ghost. Now tell me, are you ready to continue because I can find something more important to do?"

"Yeah, yeah, I just zoned out. What is my next test?"

"Now you go into that room for your awareness test."

"And what is the reason for this test?"

"Obviously to test your awareness," I asked because he didn't tell me the reason for my last test. Maybe there was something mystical about it. Ace closes the doors and immediately went to talk to Grim, "Why am I testing him? Other than me I don't know anybody who passed the first test. You didn't give me another test and you didn't give anybody else this test."

"Remember when I told you he reminds me of you?"

"Yeah."

"Ok now observe. He will go through two stages; first stage with the lights, second stage without the lights. Each stage has a set number of holographic combatants. As he takes each one down they become harder to defeat."

At that moment the test had begun. I was progressing rapidly taking each one down like a domino. It wasn't easy and it didn't get easier.

Ace was somewhat impressed, "He is skilled, but I don't see me."

"Hahaha," Grim busted out into laughter, "Wait until he goes berserk."

I finished the first stage when the lights shutoff. I didn't know what had happened.

"Now, for the moment of truth, stage two is specifically created for him. Hopefully, it triggers his rage, anger and raw emotions so you can better understand him being your partner."

The room was pitch-black. I began to hear voices taunting me. I was still unaware of what was going on. Then I was attacked. I was ignoring the voices, but as I was being attacked I was losing control. I fought as best I could without going berserks.

Ace said jokingly, "I guess he needs to be taught a little self-control."

Grim responded, "Like you have self-control."

Eventually, I lashed out with a war cry. I was struggling because I couldn't see. My emotions took over now I am suffering the consequences.

"So what do you expect me to do?" Ace asked.

"You will get him to open up. His emotions override his instincts, his common sense; the key to survival. He is afraid to let his body react freely. When he loses all control and he is in his most primitive state, his instincts takeover. His raw emotion releases a stench so potent so pure it was like a manly musk mixed with adrenaline; the rush, the power, the energy at its maximum potential. Help him reach that potential minus the fear."

Grim ended the test. It took a while, but Ace got the whole picture. Ace became curious after the test, "Was I like that, and filled with fear of being myself?"

Grim answered, "You needed an identity and that caused your rage."

Ace laughed hard, "Haha, there you go with jokes again."

"Ok so you're in denial, Anon will teach you otherwise. Believe that," Grim said it and meant it.

"Haha next you're going to tell me pigs can fly. Hahahahahaaa!!!" Ace laughed until a tear fell from his eyes. Then he went to give me the news, "How did you like stage two?"

"If you are asking how I like fighting in the dark, then I don't like it at all," I was relieved to be able to see again. Having to fight blind is not as cool as it seems.

"Were you scared?"

"Why would I be afraid of a test?"

"You know, we could have let you get beaten to death."

"Well I wasn't worried. You need me."

"Is that a fact? Wait, I know it was another joke. The bad news is you failed the test, the good news is I don't have to give you a title."

"So you're really going to call me Anon the Unknown?"

"You said Grim did everything. What you just did was for my knowledge."

"Great, but I should let you know I lied about that part, so what's really my title?"

"Your title is Anon the Unknown. Oh and I knew you were lying."

"Can't you give me another name?"

"Yeah, if you would like to be called Anon the Clown."

"Ha, nice joke. Anon the Clown hahahahahaha."

"That is what I thought. Now we have to go over protocol and then we hunt."

"Didn't you hear me? I was joking."

"According to Grim it's real."

At that time we left to go over the procedures with Grim. I was in shock. I didn't feel up to the task. I was hoping for a break or a breath of fresh air at least.

At the back of my mind I was thinking, "This can't be real. What did I sign up for?" Everything was moving too fast. They must have wanted a problem out of me. I didn't understand why I react in such a way, but it was no longer my problem; let them figure it out.

We entered Grim's office only to discover a note on his desk addressed to me. The message read, "Now that you've finished everything it is time for the real deal. Ace is your partner and I'm sure he has already informed you of your task. Do whatever it takes to get the job done. You two are partners so there is no need to hide anything from him. Be who you are. P.S. - Ace is bad with names. He may change it. –Grim the Healer." I read it aloud. Maybe Ace is better than I think.

"Great now let's gear up and *Trap the Rat*," Ace was excited to go on this task. I damn near wet my pants thinking about going on this mission. It isn't much different from before, except now I have to strike first. We were preparing for a long trip. It could take a few hours, days, months, or years.

Before we went to bed Ace said, "We need our rest so we leave at first light," he was serious at this point. He left to his room to get his rest, while I was feeling restless. Everything I experienced today flooded my mind with chaos. I was tossing and turning all night. It took longer than expected but I fell asleep. Our mission seems impossible. I believe Ace only knows a few people affiliated with G.O.D. and he's been there since day one. None of that matters anymore. The only person Ace needs to depend on is me.

Grim, he never sleeps. He's always working in his office. He finds tasks for us to complete. He has a lot on his mind even more than usual.

"It would probably help if I gave them a list of members. The only problem is every member knows of Ace as my right hand. I'll give them a list anyway. Hopefully they can identify them by their demeanor. G.O.D. has a distinct look and attitude. Whoever is trying to kill me knows my weakness. I can't hide forever I got to live too," After hours of thinking Grim decided that it would be most strategic to search for himself. I mean his transformations are flawless, what more does he need? I know you are wondering, how an angel takes human form, but that is a mystery.

Chapter 3: The Root of Deceit

Grim had a hard life. I can tell you he only did what he learned to do. The only person he looked up to banished him from heaven. God believed Grim was trying to impersonate him. He felt threatened, so he made it impossible for him to return to heaven. Since that day, Grim only did what he thought was best. He built an army to do the angel's deeds. He still acts as if he is protecting the *Gates of Heaven* by creating the *Gates of Judgment*. We followers are people who have inner hatred and have no way of releasing it. Some do alright, others can't handle it. Before meeting Grim most of us had no choice. He gave us the opportunity to make a decision. He fights for us and grants us the power to fight for ourselves. He answered our prayers. We had little comfort, if any, and we had little to no motivation; survival of the fittest.

Can you imagine being ridiculed for being all you were taught to be? Grim has no choice, but to stay in the battlefield. We put all our faith in one man who answers our prayers. He is a healer. He made music for our comfort and motivation. His music is the equivalent of the Bible. There is a basic understanding, but it is up to us to interpret the message. Grim is a fallen angel. Calling him Satan, Lucifer, or the Devil is because of ignorance. It's disrespectful, but he spares their lives. I knew who he was, but now that I'm on his side I see that he shines a bright light in dark places.

There are rumors that God is trying to destroy the reaper (Grim's title before he got banished and created an army). The reaper no longer exists, unless someone else was given that title. All I know is Grim was given a bad reputation. Everybody deserves a second chance. Why not Grim?

Chapter 4: The Core

Grim had been lost for so many years following the path like a blind man. He was blind to his responsibilities. In time he found his way through the dark. What else was there for him to unfold: life, dreams, reality; that is truth of reality? Time was the biggest setback. It was wasted without any consideration. No longer could he stay in this situation. Circumstances had to change before he ceased to exist. His life had begun as a man. It couldn't have ended at such a young age. The world was Grim's for the taking and all who want to carry it, embrace it, and build it in G.O.D.'s image.

Entry#1

Nobody listens to what I have to say. They hear what they want to hear. I shout insanity they claim I cry wolf. I speak truth they assume I'm telling fictional stories. In the beginning all was given to me. In the end I give it all back. With all my heart, body, and soul I promise never to give up until my last breath. Even then I won't give in. through pride and prejudice, love and hate, vice and virtue, the world and all things on it will be tested. There is no weak and strong only dead or alive. Either way, a life must be lived. The world believes in false hopes and words, rarely the speechless who use common sense and take matters into their own hands. Instead of reacting in applause, they react in silence and stillness.

Grim the Reaper

Entry#2 Let Me Breathe

I'm spazzing, over voicing the artist. The music had stop because I'm battling. My voice is soft and direct. I don't raise the tone for the lion in me attacks. He is defensive protecting what is his. The monkey I proclaim to be picks pockets. Let me explain. He plays on words and fucks up the land stealing info. If you truly understand take my info, ladies only. I want a nympho; I want a dominatrix, a nurse playing doctor, school teacher playing a schoolgirl. I need a geisha to marry me. I need to let loose and fuck everything. You misunderstand and I fucked your head up. Don't try to understand just ride and see, fly with me. The king wants all to shine before he dies. Bury my ashes or drown my sins because I'm coming back to haunt resurrecting just so I can perfect my stunt.

Grim the Reaper

Entry#3 Express Oneself

I'm on my way to the top. The pain I feel has gotten no better. Money is the world. My mother is dying because of it. Everything she was born with is obsolete. Kids aren't acting young as they are. Parents no longer take responsibility for their children. I grew up before I knew what life was. I'm screwed up like Frankenstein's monster. I'm a project and I knew it when I was a kid. A cloned outcast that was destined to be behind bars forever. My friends use me and my family dismissed me because I believed

I was a man. Truthfully, I was man enough to be on my own. I was shunned, abandoned, put out for wanting to hear a voice that understood other than what was echoing in my head. Did they know their voice was in my head ringing with words of criticism? No face, no body, no soul. My imagination, my daydreams, my nightmares had destroyed me for most wouldn't listen. I fought for myself and my brother. We wanted to kill each other and our mother. Now that they see the men we are it is easier. I found my voice and took control of reality. If we couldn't persist through life we as people would rot and become one. Separate we are easy targets, but as one anything is possible even eternal life.

Grim the Reaper

Entry#4 My Pain is Power

Scars show character and tell a story. Tribes purposely scarred those who proved worthy. Today we call them tattoos. The question that is generally asked is why destroy, scar, or put a brand on somebody or oneself? The answer depends on the person.

Personally I choose to use tattoos as reminders that I can see every day. Being disassociated from most people I hear more than I should. Sort of like a telepathic power or psychic ability. My daydreams and nightmares give insight and wisdom towards the future. After a while it becomes Déjà vu and reality starts to repeat itself. Your memory is screwed because some days you believe you've gone back in time. Before I knew the scars I acquired were permanent. Tattoos are also a way to cover up scars that are uncovered. A new sense of life is received from being relieved of a painful past. Presently I'm creating a new identity that better expresses me. Tattoos as I said are a reminder of who I am.

Grim the Reaper

Entry#5 The Elixir

I'm doing better than I expected. The kids are enjoying their selves and everybody is taking care of business. Hard work pays off from the moment you start to the moment you finish. No pain no gain, no effort no outcome. I am Atlas and the world is on my shoulders; the mentality I take on life isn't the same. All things are possible even bringing the dead to life. The world is yours and mine, instead of fighting it embrace it for when it dies we die with it. Never forget all things are possible; eternal life, life after death, virgins giving birth, etc.

Grim the Reaper

Entry#6

Express yourself through words, with sound, or body motion. Nobody can stop an expression. Faces, hands signals, even silence is an expression. To feel or not to feel? What is understood can be misunderstood. Let loose and live like it's your last chance. Every breath taken brings you closer to the end. Every second lived brings you closer to new beginnings. Every beginning has an end and at every end is a beginning. Those stuck in the middle don't progress; they slowly get behind and become depressed. Move forward, never look back, never forget, and stay persistent and consistent through life.

Entry#7

I'm stronger now than I was before. All my personalities are slowly coming back as one. If they had the chance they would destroy me. I'm in control and if I lose control I will use it and lose it for a limited time, for this is when I am most vulnerable. Peace, harmony and awareness; are key in winning any fight. Ignorance, vanity, and cockiness will blind and disrupt the mind and body, clouding judgment and movement. Reactions and actions need no thought. Follow your first instinct and never second guess it. Instinct is emotionless. If actions are fueled by any emotion it isn't instinct. A clear empty mind is better than a world of chaos and randomness. Instinct is chaotic info that's flows in an organized pattern. Remain calm and actions will do more than any thought or emotion.

Grim the Reaper

Entry#8

Progression in a time of depression is like laughing and crying at the same time. Pain is fuel for the fire. Today there was more interaction with the rest of the world. Feedback was a major part in it all. Ladies are feeling my vibe and pain, but still won't take me out of my zone. One night with one girl so I could let go for a moment. No guard or mask. No motive or outside influence or terrorizers; a simple night close to one another. No intercourse is necessary, but appreciated. Real love, intellectual conversation, a good time. The neighborhood is no longer silent and neither am I. My singing dancing and acting is more than they could have asked for. I still associate, but only in response to the feedback and through my frustration and to clear my mind. All this is to lift a weight I carry in my heart. The world is in my hands and I will break my back to keep it alive. Work with me and I'll work with you. As a child and now as a man I influence others young and old to enjoy life and do what is needed to make one's life as you want.

Grim the Reaper

Entry#9

Every day I find new inspiration. Last night I believed it would rain and today a light shower came. I attempted to repeat a dance move and I accomplished it. My voice, my presence and appearance is becoming more defined. No longer will I lose control without reason or notice. The world is listening and God is too. Soon I have to return to my original duties.

Grim the Reaper

Entry#10

I'm doing all I can to maintain sanity, but the man they claim I was to become is trying to provoke me. It's to the point where he breaks his own rules. He expects more of me than he does of himself. I want to fight, but there is no motive behind it other than frustration and anger. Put me in a cage match, pay for my recording, send me home, kill me, or tell me, better yet show me exactly what you want me to do. I understand subliminal messages, but my understanding isn't your understanding. I don't have a true example to follow. I'm still being lied to and cheated out of parts of my life. I'm supposed to be happy, but someone wants to steal it. I'm supposed to be away from false judgment, yet I'm in the epicenter. It's like they expect me to kill or die for a cause I don't believe in. Physically I'm free, mentally I'm free, spiritually I'm free, but I still suffer from verbal abuse and my emotions stay locked away forever. I can speak it, show it, but maintaining it isn't an ability I have. Peace has no definite emotion and neither does war. Money is the source of power and respect. I don't want material desires. It's a necessity in most cases. Until the critics see who I've truly become I must fight.

Grim the Reaper

"I have been lost for so many years following the path of a blind man. I was blind to my responsibilities as a man. In time I found my way through the dark. What else was there for me to unfold? Life? Dreams? Reality? That is truth of reality. Time was the biggest setback. It was wasted without any consideration. No longer could I stay in this situation. Circumstances had to change before my life ceased to exist. My life had just begun as a man. I couldn't have it end at such a young age. The world is mine for the taking and all who want to carry it, embrace it, and build it in God's image," Grim had an amazing idea.

Chapter 5: Rainman

The morning had come and it was time to go hunting. I had so many concerns that resonated from the night before. All I knew was we were doing Grim's work. I apologize. We were doing GOD's work. So of course I had questions, "Are we supposed to bring him back dead or alive?"

"It doesn't matter. As long as we take care of our tasks," Ace wasn't much for talking in the morning. He was also a bit of a brute. It didn't matter I had questions that needed answering.

I asked, "Does everybody have a partner?"

"Depends on the task," Ace replied with military precision.

"Has G.O.D. ever had a rivalry that ended in war?"

"No. Why do you have so many questions? I thought you didn't trust us. Why are you so interested in something you don't believe in?"

"First of all, I never said I didn't believe. Second, I am asking questions because I don't trust G.O.D. Ya'll don't need to know me, but I need to know you all." I started reading the list.

"Did it ever occur to you that we didn't say anything because we weren't ready to tell you? We don't trust you either," Ace didn't do anything, but dodge my questions.

We argued the entire time we were walking. After a while I just enjoyed annoying Ace with juvenile concerns. It was weird though. The chemistry was balanced. I mean we were complete opposites, but it felt as if we were the same person. There were distinct differences visually, mentally, etc., but we had one goal and one mission.

"Heads up! You hear that?" Ace heard something that drew his attention. It even put a smile on his face.

"Yeah, it sounds like a powwow," I knew what I had heard, but I was distraught at Ace's reaction

"Exactly," Ace said with certainty.

I didn't know the significance of what I had heard. I hoped that this was a sign our mission was coming to an end just as soon as it started. I was curious, "so why are we here?" "I've got an old friend that lives here. He may join us," Ace said. At that moment my suspicions peaked. Who is he bringing along with us? Does he follow G.O.D. as well? Then I heard Ace shout a name, "Jacob!" It was his friend he was telling me about. His name was Jacob. I can only assume they were close.

"Ace, what brings you back to this wasteland?"

"Why must we jump to the conclusion I just got here."

"I know you don't come this way for nothing. Really, what is it that you want?"

"Can we wait until after we've had a meal? My partner and I have traveled for days with little to no food or rest."

"He must have been getting on your nerves the way you are acting."

"You have no idea."

Ace and Jacob laughed together, "Hahahaaaaaa," like old friends. Jacob started speaking to me, "Hi, I'm the guy they call to put out the fires. When I dance the gods start to weep. My stomp is thunder. My clap is lightning. One snap and I can change the weather. I am Jacob the Rainman." I was done with the formal introductions, but it lets me know who was a part of G.O.D.

Chapter 6: Enlightenment

Meanwhile I made myself comfortable with the territory. I was beginning to take in the environment. At some point and time I began to feel Grim's presence. We were in sync somehow.

That is when I heard his voice, "Anon I know you hear me. Someone in the camp will attempt to take Ace's spot as my right hand. Protect him and he will do the same."

Grim and I were still talking when Ace appeared into the woods and he said, "You done talking to Grim?"

I was in suspense, unaware. I managed to recover, "yeah... yeah, how you know?"

He replied with a direct answer, "The Northern lights at the equator isn't normal."

I said, "No it isn't normal."

Ace wasn't done yet, "Are you telling me you noticed the aurora before you met Grim?" Ace looked puzzled.

Not knowing anything about it, "Yeah can't everybody? I thought, maybe, it was a telepathic portal Grim shows his followers."

Ace continued to further explain what I was experiencing, "Only a select few are connected with Grim on that level, even fewer have the ability. It is called *Enlightenment*."

The way he explained it Grim struck gold recruiting me. I didn't take tests for nothing, "Is that why I had meditation as one of my tests?"

"You should know the answer to that. Let me show you how to reach someone in private through *Enlightenment*." Ace showed me what to do, and then I copied him.

Later after I gained better control he began telling me something else, "Anon you may also speak to your enemies using the same technique. Furthermore be cautious and remember they can hear, see, and feel as you do."

At that moment it dawned on me, I could have a conversation with Jacob in private. Speaking of the devil, he had come to retrieve us from the woods,

"Can I join the party?"

Ace was reflecting on past memories of Grim teaching him, "You are special Ace. You can speak to anybody from anywhere; anybody you visualize, anybody you can feel or sense (old friends, even the deceased)," It caused Ace to hesitate before replying, "I was just demonstrating to Anon how to reach *Enlightenment*."

Jacob was excited to hear that, "Cool! He can do it too."

Ace confirmed, "Yes sir, I guess you can call him my son."

Both Ace and Jacob laughed heavily. I didn't think it was funny. Simultaneously, Jacob took us around camp so we were familiar with the area. Finally we made it to our tent.

"This is where you two will be sleeping tonight. I will have someone retrieve you when dinner is ready," Jacob left to finish his duties. Immediately, I asked Ace, "Ace, have you talked to Grim yet?"

He replied, "Not since we left him. Why?"

I told him what Grim had told me, "When we spoke he told me someone was trying to kill you."

Ace didn't seem surprised, "That's nothing new."
I was in disbelief, "I mean someone from this camp?"

"You are absolutely positive?" he said with sarcasm.

"Yes, and for some reason Jacob raises the most flags," I said with emphasis.

"Haha, do you know how long he has wanted my position? That's why he has this camp," Ace said with confidence.

I was concerned so I asked, "Didn't you tell me you can talk to your enemies as well?" Ace nodded as a response, "What if he has been reaching out to Jacob the entire time?"

Ace didn't want to listen anymore, "Let it go," he told me with a stern voice.

I knew Ace didn't want to hear anymore accusations, but there was one more thing about *Enlightenment* that I needed to know, "Is there a way to hide or change signs of communicating through *Enlightenment*?"

Ace answered, "That is a good question. The only person I've seen do it was Jacob."

"And you aren't a bit worried?" I said out of curiosity.

He said, "No."

I continued, "Has this ever crossed your mind?"

"Never, we've never broken oath since the day Grim took us in," he said once again in confidence.

I said sarcastically, "You got to be Joker."

"That I am, but I am not telling jokes. Go talk to Jacob and see for yourself."

I didn't want to hear that, but I took the time to focus on *Enlightenment*. Once I left the tent Ace spoke with Grim, "Grim, Anon is advancing fast. He senses Jacob's nervous energy as well."

Grim spoke, "Don't focus on Jacob. I talked to him before you arrived. He is held hostage by someone close to him. Reach out to him through *Enlightenment*. That way you can meet with our adversary. I fear he is merely a pawn holding our rook in place."

Ace was doing his best to hide his anger, "What do you think is the best course of action? I'm on the board too. Do I hold position or confront him directly and take him off the board?"

Grim senses that Ace is anxious so he changed plans, "Neither, it is not your turn. Plan for Jacob to betray you or give up his captor's location."

Ace felt uneasy and frustrated with Grim's decision. He said more to Grim, "One more thing, I knew Anon would have contact with you, but why does an aurora appear over him when he reaches *Enlightenment*? It was unbelievable seeing such peace and harmony."

Grim shook his head. "He is more powerful than you realized. Do you need to know how 3-way before I go?" he said sarcastically.

"No, like you said it isn't my turn." said Ace.

Grim chuckled, "Haha," just before complimenting Ace, "That's my Joker."

Chapter 7: The Way (Tao)

I had an ominous feeling that led me to believe Jacob was the conspirator. Being as I was told to let it go, I decided to join the other villagers. While amongst them one particular person caught my eye. She was a villager, but she wasn't with everyone else. She had thick, long, blue hair that looked soft as cotton and smooth as silk; dark color skin that had a trance-inducing glow; her eyes looked like big hazel gemstones; she was about four feet eleven inches and moved with grace and purity. All I know is I had begun talking in sotto voce to mask my words. As she noticed me I took steps towards her as if I were invited to meet. She laughed and approached me flirtatiously. Indeed she noticed me. Was she thinking about how admirable I was or my obsession with her? Either way, now, I'm obligated to receive her invitation.

I was love sickened with vice over virtue tied up in a fantasy. She took it upon herself to speak first, "Hi, I'm Na`ina. I noticed you sleep walking and thought I'd intervene."

I had to snap back to reality. I said, "Well I am Anon and I'm thankful for your kindness." I was stricken by her lust and glamour.

At that moment Ace noticed Na`ina with Anon and remembered to *Enlighten* Jacob. It started raining once he reached *Enlightenment*.

"Sorry to rain on your parade Jacob, but it seems Anon is getting around well."

"Rain is who you asked for. And what do you mean?"

"He met with your niece and seems to be putting the moves on her. Hahahaha…"

"Don't worry she's a heartbreaker. What was so important you had to make it rain?"

"Can you show him that *Enlightenment* trick?"
Jacob said sarcastically, "Sure are there any other secrets you want me to spill?"

"Yes, can you teach him *The Way*? He's a fireball waiting to burst. He doesn't feel 'rain' if you know what I mean."

"The only way to put out a fireball is to suffocate it or drown it. Don't worry I will bring him around."

Ace left *Enlightenment* so Jacob could *Enlighten* Anon. He said, "Anon if you are looking for me I will be by the waterfall."

Na`ina and I were out of the rain, finally, but I still had unofficial business to finish. "Hey Na`ina, I don't want to leave but I forgot I have to meet Jacob at the waterfall."

She said, "Tell my uncle don't keep you long. Dinner is cooling off and he has to bless the food with a ceremonial dance." I was so shocked I had to repeat her, "your UNCLE?"

I couldn't believe what my ears had heard. I thought dinner was done and over. Oh well, to the waterfall I went. It never stopped raining the entire time I walked. When I got there Jacob was beneath the waterfall.

"I was looking for you everywhere Jacob."

"That's not what my niece told me." Those were the last words I wanted to hear out his mouth.

"Don't tell me, she's G.O.D. too."

"God knows all," Jacob laughed out loud before he finished, "It was Joker. And make sure you finish your task before you get comfy with my niece." Almost simultaneously I had a feeling of disgust and resentment towards Ace.

Then Jacob said, "Now I brought you here because I heard you wanted to change your *Enlightenment*. So, we're going to take a swim.

"Why are we swimming in the rain?"

"Is it raining now?"

"How did you do that?"

"It is still raining. I am talking to you through *Enlightenment*."

I was still unraveling my brain beyond comprehension. The rain had completely stopped. I was more than just confused, for once, I was intrigued.

Then Jacob asked me, "Are you ready to swim now?"

I said sarcastically, "NO," then I changed clothes and eased into the water.

He continued with the lesson, "Alright now you're all in, how does the water feel?"

Was he serious? What does this have to do with the lesson? "The water feels cold and wet and shallow," I answered as best I could.

"Right, but you don't feel anything else?" he asked trying to get more out of me.

"I feel the current."

"That's it. Now let's swim."

"I don't believe the water goes deeper than two or three feet."

"It doesn't. We are taking a swim in your thoughts."

"How do you know I will be able to do what you did?"

"You can't. You may be able to change your aurora, so I will show you *The Way*."

"*The Way* to where?"

"*The Way* or *Tao* is its most known name. Taking your complex aurora and simply changing it. The only way you can do this is to be unselfish."

"What do you mean?"

"What I mean is everybody who shows a clear sign they are *Enlightened* are synced to the Earth. So synced, they can control the change. I control the water in the clouds. You control how sunlight reflects through to the Earth."

"So you brought me here for nothing?"

"Light reflects in many ways: Northern lights, rainbows…" Jacob said before I interrupted, "Great I can make a rainbow." Jacob resumed the lesson, "Yes a rainbow. What do you think the northern lights are?" Jacob asked me a rhetorical question, so I answered sarcastically, "Neon lights in the sky." Jacob wasn't having the jokes, "If you're done we can continue! With practice, yes, you can make a rainbow. You can also make the colors in the rainbow appear individually. Plus, Na`ina loves rainbows."

Dinner was ready so we couldn't do much. So Jacob and I went back to camp to bless the food and eat.

Jacob was ecstatic, "You like the food my niece prepared?"

"I thought we were going to miss it. I think I ought to live here."

"Hahahaaa… Hey Ace, you better get this joker before he takes my niece away from me."

Ace responded, "Why? I'm sure she'll break his heart."

Jacob laughed then stood and brought everyone to a whisper so he could do his ceremonial dance. The dance he did was special. Not only did it bless the food it welcomed all guests. I wasn't impressed. I was more interested in Na`ina.

After dinner Jacob and I went to the waterfall so I could take the time to understand *The Way* to reach my full potential.

"It is time to go swimming again," Jacob wasn't going to allow me to slack off not even once.

"In the water?" I had to ask we had just eaten.

Jacob was no fool, "No, you'll catch a cramp before we start. We are going to the top of the waterfall."

For hours Jacob taught me *The Way*. He critiqued and criticized everything I did until I perfected the technique. Learning *The Way* was exhausting, "How long do we have to do this?"

"Until you master *The Way*."

"You can call it *Tao* I understand."

"Okay, how about we test your strength. Reach *Enlightenment* and if I witness a change we end this session."

"Cool, so what I gotta' do?" I was naive and oblivious to my fore comings.

Jacob replied immediately, "I guess this session isn't over yet."

"What do you mean? I haven't started yet."

No change occurred as I reached *Enlightenment*. So, Jacob and I worked long days and nights until I could reach my full *Enlightened* potential.

Days passed. I was still in the same position from which we had started.

"It has been a week and nothing. When are we leaving?" I was getting irritated and impatient. I even started to believe I wasn't capable of *Tao*.

Then Ace appeared, "After you can change your *Enlightenment*. You give away your cover too easily. Do it for Na`ina. Hahaaa!!!"

"I'm taking a break," I was fed up with my progress and the technique for that matter.

"Were you going to see Na`ina?" Ace said to taunt me. He was doing his best to make me angry by laughing at me.

So I gave him a taste, "Yes, now shut up!" At that point, I left to go see Na`ina.

"Does he know your niece has been watching the entire time?"

"I know the boy is an idiot. He is doing it for selfish reasons. He doesn't understand *Tao* or the process in its entirety."

"That's why I'm the best. I have no tell"

"Yes you do."

"What is it?"

"You start smiling."

"Wow, really though?"

Na`ina stepped into the conversation, "Yep."

Ace asked her, "and what makes you an expert?"

"I know a Joker when I see one," she said with confidence then smiled as if she were laughing.

Ace said to Jacob, "You are right. Na`ina is a heartbreaker." Then continued to speak to Na`ina, "Can you help him use *Tao* properly, please?"

She answered, "Of course I can."

"Thank you," Ace was extremely grateful to have some assistance. So she went to find me and give me the boost I needed. Meanwhile Ace and Jacob spoke with Grim who had *Enlightened* them.

"Ace! Jacob! Be on the lookout for your fellow mates. They aren't pleased. They have some regrets about joining G.O.D. Take care of it please. I'm meeting the rebel leader. Understood?"

Ace said, "Understood." At the same time Jacob said, "I'm on it." Ace stayed *Enlightened* for he had more concerns, "What about Anon? His status is unknown."

"Good, you have a secret weapon," Grim said confidently.

Ace wasn't at all pleased. He shook his head like it was a bad joke, but he knew Grim was serious.

Ace left and asked Jacob a question, "How long do you think Anon will take before he comes to reality?"

"Never," Jacob answered.

"Well, I guess my secret weapon is still a prototype."

"That he is Ace. That he is."

In the meantime, I was still looking for Na`ina. Then she taps me on the shoulder, "Where have you been? Shouldn't you be with my uncle?" she was concerned.

"Yes, I had to take a break and clear my head. This *Tao* thing is not easy." I was frustrated.

"I will give you this fruit and then you have to go back, ok?" She was really trying to persuade me to go back.

"But why? I don't know what *Tao* is or how to use it."

I had given up all hope. I shook my head, sat down, and looked at the ground. At that moment, Na`ina sat next to me and gave me a kiss on the cheek. I was confused. What happened? I turned and looked at her as she spoke, "You ready now?" I said nothing to her. I stood up smiled and nodded. She knew I was ready. Then we walked to the waterfall together.

Ace and Jacob were still waiting at the waterfall for me to return. They were anxious to see if I was going to return.

"You think he's going to come back soon? I think you freed me of this curse," Ace said out of spite.

Jacob was right beside him with his arms crossed, "Just wait. If he is as mesmerized by my niece as she is attracted to him, they both will be back."

"For the sake of Grim I hope you are right because if you ask me he's worthless without any form of camouflage."

Ace and Jacob left discouraged. Somehow they crossed paths with Na`ina and I as they were going back to camp. With Na`ina by my side I walked with intensity and vigor. I had nothing to say.

Ace and Jacob stopped a few feet in front of me, but I kept walking with a sense of determination, pride, and honor. Na`ina watched alongside Ace as Jacob followed me. There were no regrets, no worries, no distractions, and most of all no more selfishness.

It was almost as if I understood *The Way*. So hours turned to days and days turned to weeks. For a whole month I simply and unselfishly perfected *Tao*. Before I knew there was no tell sign I was *Enlightened*.

"Anon you've come far. Now you are just as good as I am," then Ace switched to Jacob, "Jacob I know you have a village, but will you join us on this journey?"

"There is no one to lead or protect the village, so I must stay. This is my task. Once you finish yours you may come back and celebrate again," Jacob said with a grin.

"Awesome."

"You too Anon."

Then he wrapped his arm around his niece. She said, "Yea because you have to come back for me," then she blew me a kiss.

Ace and I said our goodbyes and went about our task.

Ace and I accomplished a goal; rather I had reached my potential. I was in control. Even though I found my way, everybody was still worried I will lose my way of focus and security.

Chapter 8: Gangster Mentation

Until now, Grim had been walking. He met with Roger the Rebel in an underground saloon. It was Roger's secret hangout so to speak. There were waitresses, strippers, a huge bar, private seating, and live music. If only it wasn't filled with the stench of tobacco smoke and spilled liquor. All of a sudden a figure appears, "Nice of you to have me at your personal estate." Grim just walked up to the table where Roger was sitting, "Rebel don't like pleasantries, so what special task you need me to sabotage?"

"How do you know what I'm about to ask you to do? Am I that shallow or just transparent?"

"I just knew you would come to me one day with something a little more destructive in mind. Plus, when do we ever meet at my saloon?"

"OK, you got me so I'll skip to the point. Ace is on his way to get me again. This time I need you to end his life."

"Is Rainman involved?

"No, I have his camp at my disposal."

"So why do you need me again?"

"I don't. You want his position and he wants me dead, simple as that."

"OK, as long as I'm not restricted in my means of killing him."

"Do as you wish. One more thing, he has a partner I paired with him."

"Why would you do that?"

"He must die too. Anybody who assists them must die as well."

"Roger is at your service. Task accepted."

Roger began his chant of enlightenment to reach his team, "An eye for an eye, a hand for a hand, Enlighten me as I call my clan…"

He reached three people; Calypso, Pierre and Pigeon, "Come back to the spot we got a major task."

Bad news was sure to come with those four together. If there were any idiots that needed to die it was them.

Our worst nightmare came true, but this wasn't the first time Ace had to fight his own. Pierre, Calypso, and Pigeon walked straight in, "Fellas, our moment has come!" Roger said with extreme enthusiasm. Each one took a seat alongside Roger and ordered a drink.

"I'll have the *devil's cut* of bourbon," said Pigeon.

Then Pierre ordered, "Give me the same and a shot of rum."

Lastly Calypso ordered, "I'll take whatever knocks an elephant out… and a glass of milk."

After everybody received there drinks Roger spoke, "Remember that intricate plan we had set up?"

Calypso responded, "For whom? We have so many."

"Yea, my memory is not that sharp anymore," Pigeon added.

"The one for Joker," said Roger.

Calypso was getting frustrated, "I thought that was for Grim…?"

Roger sighed, "YOU FOOL!!!! It's for Ace and Grim."

"Do you think Grim is that smart? How do you know he won't find out? And what's intricate?" Calypso asked without thinking twice about what he said. "Listen you fool he won't and that's it. We are taking over as G.O.D." Roger was enraged to hear he was doubted.

Immediately, they went to work. Pierre took the first approach, "It's time for Skrull to break the rules."

"I should've made the plans myself…" Calypso's thought. Pierre did what he had planned to do. Within an hour he left a trail of destruction then disappeared. The village was on fire; the people were charred, animals slaughtered, blood trails and pools were the only evidence life existed. Pigeon did the same in another village almost as a parade to guide us to their hideout. The stench was nauseous, the sight was blinding, dark, skies filled with scavengers, the cacophonous sound of screaming people being eviscerated, you could taste death in the air," Calypso's senses flooded his thoughts.

Roger stared deep in thought, "Now, we sit back and use our heads. We can be G.O.D. once we finish this task and take out Grim. Now let me think." He sat for hours thinking while the others made their way back to the hideout. Roger yelled, "AWWW!!! MY HEAD HURTS!" He started having second thoughts, "I knew I should have let the fool make the plans."

Truthfully Calypso is the leader. He has all the ideas. The other three just act inspired or consumed in thought. Roger owns the spot, Calypso makes the plans, Pigeon and Pierre follow the leader. Enough about those fools, Calypso is a true mastermind. Meanwhile, Calypso started making plans of his own. He was planning for Grim.

"Ok. Now, I *enlighten* Ace," Calypso decided to make his move, "Ace, I need your help finding who destroyed the villages earlier today."

"What does Roger have planned?" Ace asked suspiciously.

Calypso taunted Ace, "Who knows? We need a detective right away. Know any other good ones?"

Ace chuckled, "You must be a fool to think I'm falling for that trap."

"It could have a clue to our enemy. I'm no scientist, but I know somebody is trying to takeover G.O.D. If it is true it is worth wasting time," Calypso told Ace.

Ace said furiously, "You fool…"

"BYE," Calypso's last word before leaving *Enlightenment.*

Immediately, Ace summoned me, "Anon, we got a lead. Remember the idiots I told you about?"

"Maybe…" I said mindlessly.

"Well you are about to meet them soon,"

Chapter 9: Grief Mountain

"Ay, It has been a long journey, but I'm here; the mountains of grief," Grim said feeling relieved. There were bones, tombstones, urns and ashes hidden in the mist. Grim maneuvered the mountains to find a path. The path had a stone doorway which leads to a cave underneath. The cave was filled with life; green grass, clear waters, vibrant plants, and an abundance of food. It was the epitome of an oxymoron; a perfect picture in fact.

Grim read an inscription on the walls of the cave, "What is on the inside is hidden by my outside. Nobody has been inside this cave in any lifetime." He continued speaking, "I own their souls. I own their image."

"The majority of the bones are unfortunate wanderers. It wasn't the eye that can see, but the bones and bare structure that lives within us." The doorway he entered is hidden. Only those with the power of *Enlightenment* could see it was the only route.

The mountain of grief is Grim's sanctuary. For others, the mountains were a wasteland where no life existed. The sight itself puts fear in your heart. Grim would wait here until it was time for a resurrection.

Chapter 10: Coocandoo Heights

I asked, "So how close are we to the next village? Food, a bed, and a shower would be nice. It has been days since we have seen any indictor of a threat, better yet, civilization."

"Bye, you can go back whenever you are ready. I'm not your babysitter," Ace said with no concern.

"I'm just saying; where are we going?" I was concerned.

Ace decided it was time to tell me, "Coocandoo Heights is where Grim rescued me and Jacob. It is also a battleground between G.O.D., the people, and the idiots (petty thieves and wannabe gangsters). Treat this place as if you have lived here your entire life, otherwise it will become your grave. We are here."

Ace and I came to a bridge that was built, in addition to the city, to transport goods.

Back at the camp Na'ina asked Jacob, "Uncle, do you think they know?"

"Of course they do. Hope it ends soon," he replied

Pigeon appears in Coocandoo, "Before I wreak havoc here in Coocandoo I'll have a drink and a dance at the strip club."

Pigeon is an act now asks later kind of guy. He is not very bright. Brute force is his only advantage.

"This place feels like home," I felt a sense of security.

Ace says comically, "You are a wannabe gangster."

"Yea and you are a petty thief," I snapped.

"Alright this is our stop for now. Hopefully nothing happens until… NEVER," Ace said before he walks into the hotel.

We were at a hotel named "Desirea". Ace had a friend that owned the hotel named Lisa. We walked up to the counter to speak with Lisa, "Hi, can you tell Lisa her friend Ace is here to see her." The clerk went to retrieve her.

"Why are we here? Is this a gentleman's club too?" I asked out of spite.

Lisa steps in, "Hey Ace, is this your brother?"

"No, thank goodness. He is just my partner."

"Don't worry that is all we have in common. How are you, I'm Anon. It is nice to meet you."

"Lisa, and likewise," she moved on to the purpose of the visit, "So, I am guessing you both need rooms."

"Yes we need shelter. Can you hook me up?"

"You got the funds I got the rooms."

"Really? We are searching for someone we have yet to identify. I'm talking Coocandoo apocalypse."

Lisa hesitated after taking a long time to think, "Ok three nights and that's it."

Ace smiled ear to ear, "I love you so much Lisa."

"I ain't your girlfriend no more stop kissing ass. If you really loved me you wouldn't have joined GOD. Good thing too. I found strength on my own."

"Aww you still care, who knew."

I was getting sick of the intimacy. Lisa was a hardcore warrior. Sensitive wasn't a word used lightly around her.

"Alright room 28231 two beds, one full bath, kitchen storage, the works," Lisa led us to our room.

"The executive suites as usual; want to share a bed?" Ace asked.

"Ha, funny. I didn't then and I won't now," Lisa hands Ace the key and walks us in.

Right as she walks out the door he commented, "You know you cried in my arms every night." Ace locked Lisa out of the room. He knew what was about to come. Behind the door he made fake cries mocking her. Then she opens the door,

"Excuse me who run this hotel?" Ace dropped to his knees pleading forgiveness. "What I thought! I will come by to check on you. Make sure you ain't breaking my rooms," Lisa said sternly. "As will I just to bother in the meantime," Ace said in a soft voice.

"Wow!!! I puked on your bed. Whatever you just did is some intoxicating stuff," I jokingly said in an ignorant way.

"Get ready we aren't gonna stay here all day. This is home, but like I said danger breeds here. Would you like to go to the strip club? I know a way we can sneak through the back. Or, you can go with me and meet the folks," I didn't have a choice.

"I don't need a sweaty, gold digging woman to please me. I need a real genuine woman. Let's go meet the folks." I started talking to myself, "I don't want to meet the folks either. I just wanna get away and complete this task."

We walked into the club down the street, "Hey Vanessa," Ace was speaking with one of the bartenders at the club.

"Hey Ace, When did you get back in town?"

"Yesterday, did you hear any rumors?"

"Well I heard Grim was the source of chaos throughout all of the land. And…" Ace cuts Vanessa short, "HOLD UP! HOLD UP! HOLD UP! Who told you?"

"You know dumb dumb and dumber," Ace nods, "well they can't keep their mouths shut. As a matter of fact the saloon isn't far from here." Vanessa began to explain the location, "On the outskirts of town there is a desert. Follow the cacti and stay away from the scorpion caves."

Chapter11: Saloons Lagoons and Baffoons

"Alright let's create more chaos," Pigeon gets ready to do his part. He zips his pants up, pushed the stripper out the way and went about his business. On his way out the door he spots Joker. He couldn't *Enlighten* anybody as a precaution of its effects, so he snuck out the back door.

"How hard was that? We got everything we needed," Ace said with accomplishment.

I had nothing to say. I was focused on the task. Meanwhile, Pigeon followed us out of town.

It is now sundown, the air is cold and all life appeared.

I asked Ace, "You see the Jackrabbit?" Anon asked Ace

"Yea. And snakes. And scorpions. But no cactus. What is your point?" Ace wasn't amused. By the time he looked up again I disappeared. "Where the hell are you?" Ace was feeling confused. I disappeared for five minutes leaving Ace in the same spot.

"See it now…" I had a jackrabbit, two snakes, and five scorpions. "Dinner, I'm hungry. We should go this way. Also the scorpion cave is underneath is treading softly."

We set up camp, started a fire, and then planned our next move. I was prepared, "We should leave as soon as we eat. The animals are all going the same direction as the cacti…"

"Because it is the main source of water. Anything else smart ass?" Ace interrupts rudely. That's when he noticed something strange in the distance. Pigeon was trying to signal the gang. "We must be close. We have an unfriendly visitor," Ace informs me.

Pigeon held his position and watched the site. I was preparing the food to cook, so I stayed. Ace left to go hunting.

"Ok, Ace is going to hunt, so I'll study this kid," Pigeon was taking notes naive to Ace's location. "Ace has been gone for over thirty minutes now. Where is he?" Pigeon was beginning to worry. Then Ace puts a sword at his back, "I'm here." Instantly Pigeon throws dirt in his face and hides.

Ace *Enlightened* me, "Be ready. One of those idiots is out here." Pigeon started talking to himself, "It's not time to kill them, yet I don't care. I could lead G.O.D. This time is my time to step up. Fuck a plan!" He arms himself with a long sword and greets Ace, "I am Pigeon the Raptor; A prehistoric predator, a forgotten evil. I exist to kill and destroy. The Devil cut and carved me himself. You should call your partner to help you."

"You know who I am, I know who you are. You don't deserve a fair fight or an introduction from me. Where is your gang? Who is calling the shots?" Ace was all business.

"Haha, you are a Joker," Pigeon states.

Ace and Pigeon started trading blows with their swords. Chips of metal shards were slashed off with each offense. This progressed for ten minutes.

"For a killer you sure are weak," Ace taunted Pigeon.

"I am not weak!! Ahh…" Pigeon grunted.

The moment Pigeon yelled in frustration Ace cut him ten times.

"Now that I disarmed you tell me or you die in the desert," Ace ordered Pigeon to inform G.O.D. of their plans. Pigeon kept screaming in pain and terror. Then he fell to the ground. I landed a fatal blow on Pigeon, "I can't eat in peace. He was screaming. He deserved to die."

Ace thought, "He got what he wanted."

Rainman chants from his village, "Somebody is stealing from us, but I don't know who. I got an eye on my forehead, so I can soul search you. Rainman calling ALL EYES ON YOU."

"This is by far the most unusual of circumstance," Ace said thinking hard.

"What do you mean? I killed him," I didn't understand the importance of the battle.

Meanwhile, a woman appears at the entrance to the cave on Grief Mountain. Ace was subconsciously aware of the situation through his *Enlightenment.*

"*I see the grief, find the path... To life and death at peace,*" she quoted a mythical verse.

I asked, "You awake Ace?!?!?"

"Yea I just saw a woman on a mountain again," this wasn't the first time this place was seen by Ace and I.

"Are we talking about the same woman?"

"Yes Anon."

"Magnificent, you have found the place where I lay to wither," said Grim.

"Of course I created this place for you, Grim," said the woman.

"Have you? Was this your return; to be Queen Almighty, the ruler of souls, the one who sees all? Sheira?"

"You know I can steal each piece of you and hide them from you forever?"

"Ha, I'd like to see that. But for now, what info do you have for me?"

"Nothing, you know all I know Grim."

"Have you mastered your *Manipulation of Enlightenment*? It would be of great use to me."

"No I have not. That is not why I am here. My brother is dead and I sense Ace knows I'm here with you as well."

"Don't worry he is still unaware. He sensed when I stepped through the gates as well. It was his *Enlightenment* that brought this to life, if I recall."

"It was my ritual!!! You know what I had to go through to protect you from this place? This is the place of your demise. We saw it together remember Grim?" Sheira said sobbingly.

"I remember…" then Sheira walks to Grim and they hug.

Chapter 12: Back to the Problem

"Have you seen Pigeon?" Pierre was starting to wonder. "Naw I haven't, probably still at the strip club," said Roger. "You sent him to the strip club? We're supposed to destroy the cities," Pierre was frustrated. "Pierre you do more than enough damage. You burned everybody in the village and the surrounding buildings. What more do you think we need to do?" he asked Pierre with a serious look. Pierre replied, "I don't know... Lay waste to all who resist our strength."

"Due time. Where is Calypso? He should be back," Roger was starting to get irritated.

"What is he doing?" Pierre asked.

"I don't know. He is supposed to be following you," said Roger.

"Me? What is the reason?" Pierre asked. He continued speaking, "I'm the most valuable here. I have to be worth something."

"You have one point I have ten thousand points," Roger said to shut him up.

"I have a lesson for you," Grim says to Sheira.

Sheira and Ace both reply, "What is it?"

Grim gave Sheira a task, "Kill me if you must; if you can. If that is what you must do."

Grim was only talking to Sheira, but Ace was able to see and listen in on the conversation. "Whoa, I see now," Ace said in shock.

"Aww I found it finally. Is it done?" Calypso asked glad he found the hidden location.

"Yes, we have a distraction plan. Now we need to lure Grim," Roger said informing them of the plan.

"I didn't see you," Pierre said angrily.

"You did everything. You destroyed a poor, weak town. I saw everything you did," is what Calypso said in confidence.

"Great, let us move on," Roger was ready to put their plan in motion.

Ace said to me, "Anon we must find Grim." Suddenly Grim *Enlightens* Ace, "Ace I'm here. Don't come looking for me. I'm regenerating from my battle. I seduced my opponent."

"Fine keep me posted," Ace said.

I asked, "What happened?"

"Nothing just a scorpion you forgot," Ace said as he spots a scorpion.

"Huh," I yelled as Ace kills a scorpion.

"Ok now kill more I'm starved," my stomach started growling.

"Did you do that on purpose?" Sheira asks Grim.

"Yes because I saw into your soul and used your power my dear. We are one yet again. Be aware for Ace is all knowing with the right motivation," Grim replied.

Calypso *Enlightens* Ace, "Ace did you kill Pigeon?"

"Yes, he tried to follow us when I found him," Ace replied confirming Calypso's suspicion.

"Alright keep me posted," Calypso said to Ace.

"You're the bad guy not me," Ace said feeling annoyed.

I questioned Ace, "You hungry?"

"Yea," Ace said as he sat to eat dinner. We ate then rested till sunrise.

Morning comes when Jacob *Enlightens* Ace, "Ace, where are you?"

"The outskirts of Coocandoo. What's up?" Ace asked politely.

"I'm joining you shortly. Grim is the only threat we have to face," Jacob replied.

Ace was confused, "You must explain yourself! He saved us both."

Jacob continued to speak, "He set us up. We are only fighting ourselves. I couldn't tell you that at first."

"You know I can't allow you to harm Grim. This isn't the right time. Even if you are telling the truth, we have to do as he says. He has those idiots doing mass destruction," Ace said.

"Say no more. I'm on the way," Jacob said as he left to meet him.

"So now he chooses to join us, great," I was being sarcastic.

Ace said, "We should wait. He can bring us good fortune and plentiful rain, so we can drink and feast like kings."

Jacob rushed to meet them. Meanwhile, as Sheira leaves the cave, Grim was rejuvenating himself. He started to grow flesh on his bones.

All of a sudden Calypso, Pierre, and Roger come across Pigeon's body.

Calypso said, "Let's move on. See the corpse?"

"Yea let's go," Pierre said with no concern.

"Not yet. He was stabbed in the back. The only way that would have happened is if he had two opponents. He loved uneven battles. Usually in his favor, but still... we have to find these people and kill Grim in the process," said Roger taking charge.

Finally Jacob met up with me and Ace at the hotel. Sheira was in the woods picking herbs to satisfy Grim's recovery. Suddenly, she is attacked by wandering animals. She didn't want to kill them, so she deflected each one as they attacked. Next she blows dust in the air and disappears in the midst with the herbs she gathered to aid Grim as he escapes mummification. This is a problem. Why would Grim give her the task of killing him?

Ace starts thinking out loud, "Grim wants to end the fighting, but won't do a task. Unless, he doesn't want to participate in the dirty work any longer. He wants to control everything without interference." Then he starts brainstorming with Jacob. He still didn't want to believe anyone. Everybody was blaming Grim, but he hasn't done anything but lend a hand. He can't know everything. He can only assume and use his wisdom and intuition.

Now, Grim is waiting for Sheira so he can bathe and cleanse as a mortal being. The last thing she needed to harvest was Anon's blood.

Chapter 13: Making Arrangements

Jacob steps in the hotel and greets Lisa, "Hey Lisa, where is Ace." She replied, "Same room we used to use."

"Thanks," he said politely.

"Bye," Lisa replied.

He went upstairs to the room and knocked. Ace answered the door, "Who is it?"

Jacob said, "Rainman here."

"Come on in," Ace says locking the door behind him. "Tell me, why does everyone want to blame Grim for their own issues?" Ace asked.

Jacob replied, "He wants to be the ultimate ruler, remember?"

"We are G.O.D. remember? We are his children as well as his army. We could take control of this situation and tasks given to change the world as G.O.D. planned. We still don't know where he is hiding. I saw, but not clearly," Ace said.

"Those dreams again?" Jacob assumed.

"Yes this time Grim was in danger. A woman was there to kill him," Ace said.

"He speaks directly to us. Remember, he knows all," Jacob said with caution.

Ace snapped, "As do I. Visions, Deja vu, and coincidences are close in relations."

"Believe me my brother in arms. He can control anyone by giving them false sight," says Jacob.

"Calypso seems to think the same," says Ace.

"Ya'll were supposed to kill them. What more do you need?"

"Let's find Grim and question him ourselves."

A traveler comes into the town yelling, "We are here!"

The traveler was passing through, so he took his time to prepare himself for his journey in Coocandoo Heights.

"We have a ride now," says Jacob.

"What?" Ace said feeling confused.

"I'll be back," then Jacob left to speak with the traveler and arrange transportation, "Sir would you mind helping me and my friends back home? I can guarantee safe travels."

The traveler said, "My name is Jogo and I would be happy to give you and your friends a ride."

On Grief Mountain Sheira appears in the cave, "Should I go extract Anon's blood or wait until he dies?"

Grim was more interested in the water, "This water feels real."

Sheira yelled, "Hello!"

Grim replied, "If you can do it yes, otherwise wait. I want to keep this place sacred and untainted by death. Arrange travel back home and destroy it before Ace and Anon go back."

Sheira had a week's journey home. But they didn't know Jacob was with them.

"Ready to go back?" Jacob asked.

"We still have those idiots to deal with," said Ace.

I stepped into the conversation, "You said Calypso is keeping tabs, let's recoup until they come to us."

"We have to end them now!" Ace exclaimed.

"They are nothing. Grim is the target," said Jacob trying to persuade Ace.

Ace said with anger, "They aren't with Grim, we are. If you are coming with us great, if not, see you later."

This was a major dilemma. Ace knows the truth, but he serves for his purpose; to assist humanity and all of life's existence.

"I can hangout for a while and wait. It is a five day trip and I'm exhausted," said the traveler.

"Let's go to this saloon and find them. This is a task so let's do this," Ace said ready to finish his task.

They left that evening in search of the saloon. Subsequently, Sheira had left at the same night, only she didn't understand Grim's reason for such destruction. If you destroy the

Gates of Judgment the world would live forever along with all life on it.

After two days journey in the desert they found the saloon. It appears to have been abandoned.

"I know those idiots left a clue here," said Ace.

There was nothing there to discover, so we headed back home. All of a sudden Jogo appears outside the saloon.

Jogo introduced himself, "I didn't know you two were brothers. I am Jogo the Traveler. I roam as a prophet of G.O.D. doing deeds and tasks for those in need."

A stranger appears, "how are you all? Why are you here? This belongs to my brothers who aren't here."

Ace started talking, "We are here searching for them. I'm Ace." The stranger made a bird call and his squad surrounded them. There were thirty of them all together; each with a face of disgust and the adrenaline of a predator.

The stranger spoke again, "We have orders to kill you all." That moment he attacked Ace. Jacob, Jogo, and I made advances towards our opponents. Everybody was facing multiple combatants at once. They were all moderate to high skilled fighters; none of which had the ability to kill. We fought them for an hour, disarming and knocking everybody out at once.

"That was odd," said Jacob.

"Yes I thought G.O.D. was all good," said Jogo.

"That is those idiots fault. They will die soon enough," said Ace

"Still, want to go back home? To protect the gates, that is?" asked Jacob.

"Yes, as much as I'd like to wait, someone we trust must be there. So we all must go," said Ace.

Chapter 14: Battle for the Gates

It had been a week before Sheira arrived at our home. She took her time going through each chamber making sure it was clear. Then she *Enlightened* Grim, "I'm here. Do you want the gates destroyed?"

He replied, "Mortal judgment is becoming more advanced. We can rebuild the gates. It has only brought pain exhaustion and frustration."

"So be it. How do I destroy it?" asked Sheira.

"Walk into the gates and trap a soul. You will awaken with me," said Grim.

She asked, "Is there any other way?"

"Bind your blood into a key and lock it. It may take a few days and we can make use of the gates later. I'd rather rebuild with you beside me," said Grim. Sheira took her time making an unbreakable key to match its lock.

"How would you like to improve your visions?" asked Grim.

Sheira was confused, "What do you mean?"

"Predicting the future; fortune telling," said Grim.

"Then I wouldn't need to destroy the gates. This is for your protection," said Sheira.

She continued making the key. She left and everyone started to *Enlighten* Grim. They were concerned because the doors were locked and they couldn't get in. Eventually, they broke the doors. Sheira was there waiting for them. One by one she took each opponent down. No words were exchanged. All of a sudden it became dead silent, when Sheira started chanting her name, "Sheira Sheira Sheira Sheira…" Then everyone dropped dead. She had hypnotized everyone and slit their throats in the process.

"Grim I killed your army. I am ready to learn now," Sheira said to Grim.

"Ok, now destroy the entrance and come to me. We will rebuild and use the gate later. Eternal life will be our creation," said Grim. It took two days, but Sheira made a key using her own blood and locked the *Gates of Judgment.*

"You still want me to destroy the gates?" asked Sheira. "Do as you see fit my dear," Grim said softly.

"Are we close? I don't remember it taking this long," I was feeling drained.

"We are here," Shouted Jogo.

"Where?" I asked. Jogo responded, "The backdoor. Only I can use it. It leads to my secret room."

Ace *Enlightens* Grim, "Grim, we are entering the backdoor. Do you need us to get anything?" Grim didn't reply. "Grim!! Let's hurry he must be in trouble," Ace said feeling worried.

Next there was a loud boom and the building was crumbling from the explosion. Then Jogo screamed, "Go back out the door, quickly!"

"Is everyone safe...? Good, let's try the front this time," said Ace. "Look that woman just left," Ace said as he spotted her.

I said, "I got her," as I ran to capture her.

"No, Jacob goes to her," said Ace then I stopped. Jacob replied, "On it."

She had disappeared in the bushes. Jacob lost sight of her, "I lost her. She destroyed our home. Do you think Grim was there?"

"No, he would've killed her," said Ace. Then Ace *Enlightens* Grim, "Grim, our home has been destroyed."

"I know. I sent someone to destroy it," said Grim.

"Why?" Ace said warily.

"I'm rebuilding the gates," said Grim.

"Why her?" asked Ace.

"She shares the same power as you," said Grim.

"Why destroy home and the *Gates of Judgment*? Why not teach me so I may protect you?" asked Ace.

Grim replied, "The gates are fine and soon you will see our creation."

Ace continued and asked grim, "Answer me this; is it true you sent Roger, Calypso, Pigeon, and Pierre on a rampage?"

"Yes," said Grim confirming what Ace had heard.

"Why shouldn't I kill you?" asked Ace.

"I am G.O.D. I know all. Kill me and you lose your *Enlightenment* and your visions," said Grim.

"I will find you and I will kill you," said Ace.

"So be it. Maybe you should wait until the *Gates of Heaven and Hell* open," said Grim.

"Maybe I will, then we can have our last meeting and you can finally rest peacefully," said Ace.

Chapter 15: Back to Life

Grim had finished regenerating on Grief Mountain. He was made of flesh and blood yet again.

"Ahhh… I breathe again. I feel rejuvenated. Now I may touch what I please. I can be amongst humans as myself."

In the meantime, Sheira was headed back to Grief Mountain to help create *The Gates of Heaven and Hell*.

"I forgot to steal their souls."

Ace, Jacob, Jogo, and I were ready to search for Grim. "We need to track that woman. Any suggestions?" Ace asked.

I said, "Ask Grim."

I left to go *Enlighten* Grim. Meanwhile, Ace Jacob and Jogo were coordinating a plan of attack.

"We still have those idiots to confront," said Ace.

"Let's hunt them and torture them until they squeal," said Jogo.

"We have yet to identify their location. One of their members is gone, so they will want revenge," said Jacob.

I *Enlightened* Grim, "Tell us where you are; show Ace your location. Tell us the location of Calypso, Pierre, and Roger."

Grim replied, "They are on their way to kill you now. Have you heard of Grief Mountain?"

I said, "No."

"You must go by yourself. My plan is to open *The Gates of Heaven and Hell*," said Grim.

I asked, "Why me?"

Grim said, "I need your blood. It is pure."

I asked, "Let's say I believe you, what is in it for me?"

"Eternal life; you become immortal as I have," said Grim.

I asked, "All I have to do is give you my blood?"

"Yes," said Grim.

I asked, "Ok, how do I find you?"

Grim said, "Find Sheira. She will bring you to me."

Then Grim *Enlightens* Sheira, "Sheira find Anon and bring him to me. He has offered himself willingly."

"As you wish. Lead him to the water well in Finesia. I will be waiting there in the underground," said Sheira.

Grim *Enlightened* me with clues to find Sheira, "Riddle me this, what runs but never walks?"

I replied, "Water."

Grim gives me another clue, "I'm not doing good I'm doing…"

I replied again, "well." Grim continued, "Go to Finesia and meet Sheira underground.

Ace noticed I was missing, "Where is Anon?" he asked.

"See I should've followed him," said Jacob feeling disappointed.

"I'll *Enlighten* him... No luck," said Jogo.

"It's ok we will find him. Let's head back to the hotel," said Ace.

A few days went by before they made it to the hotel. "You got my money?" asked Lisa.

"Uh, yes I do actually, I saved your town," said Ace as he smiled convincingly.

"Ok, you can have the room for two more days," said Lisa.

Everyone simultaneously thanked Lisa for the room and went upstairs. Meanwhile I made it to Finesia and found the tunnel that led to Sheira, "I'm Sheira, come with me. We are going to a sacred place I created in Grief Mountain."

"Let's go after Ace while Grim is in hiding," said Calypso. Then he asked Roger, "Do you want to go home?"

Roger replied, "Yea sounds good."

Pierre, Roger, and Calypso made their way home. "Wow, Grim must be buried underneath," said Roger.

"I told you let's go after Ace," said Calypso.

So they made plans to kill Ace. Sheira and I arrived at Grief Mountain. Ace, Jacob, and Jogo were still clueless as to where I was located. As for Grim he was feeling rejuvenated and energized. He was still amazed to be back to his former self. He was ready to carry out G.O.D.'s orders. "Wait until Sheira gets back. She will have no choice but to bow before me," said Grim talking to him.

"Anon, we have a long journey about three days. Or you can give me your blood now," said Sheira hoping to take my blood immediately.

I said, "No thank you. I want to see Grim first."

Sheira said, "So it shall be as you wish."

Chapter 16: Great Betrayal

Calypso *Enlightens* Ace, "Ace, where are you?"

Ace was still unsure whether to trust Calypso, "None of your business."

"If you want me dead I can always give you my location," said Calypso taunting Ace.

"Give me your location," said Ace with a serious tone.

"We're headed nowhere. Want to meet in Finesia?" asked Calypso.

Ace responded, "Sure."

Calypso jeered at Ace, "And Ace…"

"What," Ace asked sarcastically.

"Don't forget who is on your side," said Calypso.

Calypso didn't reveal Roger's plan to Ace. He merely set a trap for Roger and Pierre.

Finesia was a common place to handle business. It is a beautiful place; all sorts of animals living amongst humans, a variety of colorful plants, and the people are always friendly. But deep underground only a few dare to venture. It was an underground labyrinth filled with dead ends.

I asked Sheira a question, "Do you want Grim dead?"

She replied, "Grim is already dead."

I added, "I mean no longer of this world, buried."

"He is already dead," she said again. She was getting annoyed and ready to kill me. But days went by and then we arrived at Grief Mountain. It thundered like crashing boulders and whirlwinds; they were eroding the wasteland as the lightning struck. Still, we went to go meet Grim. "Wow, Grim couldn't change this place?" he asked prematurely. "But I did, follow me," she said calmly.

"Guys we're going to Finesia to finish my task. Hopefully we get clues to find Anon," said Ace.

"I don't like this," said Jogo.

"What do you mean?" asked Ace

"I mean Calypso sounds like a snake. Only looking out for himself," said Jogo.

"I agree," said Ace then he continued, "But he has only helped me since the task started."

"Maybe you should fight him Jogo," said Jacob.

Jogo replied, "I will."

Ace *Enlightened* me, "Where are you?"

I said, "I can't tell you yet. I'm soul searching right now,"

Ace asked, "Why?"

I said, "Grim is my concern. I'm doing a check on him."

"Ok see you soon. Peace is with you." said Ace.

"Anon is with Grim," said Ace to Jacob and Jogo.

"Did he say that?" asked Jacob.

Ace replied, "I have a good feeling."

Chapter 17: The Donor

Sheira recited the verse, "*I see the grief, find the path... to life and death at peace.*"

"Wow this place is ridiculous. You did this?" I asked Anon.

"Yes, and with your help we can build the gates," said Sheira.

"Yes we can," said Grim. He continued, "We can send people to the *Gates of Judgment* and bring them back as we please. *The Gates of Heaven and Hell* is what it will be called."

"But why?" asked Anon.

"Because G.O.D. rules over all so we control the world and how it rotates," said Grim.

I asked, "What about the conscience minded people?"

"We are the conscience minded people. Everyone else is under our control," said Grim.

"I can't let you do this," then Sheira cut me and took my blood. I was screaming in pain from the blow.

"Thanks for the donation," said Grim. Then Sheira knocked me out, tied and locked me up.

"Now you see what I have done for you," said Grim.

Sheira replied, "You put me in control of your fate yet again."

"Yes my dear. Anything you want is all yours. Now, you can do your ritual and open the gates again. Or, you can lock the *Gates of Judgment* forever."

"I need Ace for that. I thought since it was his blood that opened the gates, his soul should destroy them. But I believe the gates should be opened, so let's begin," said Sheira.

For hours Sheira worked to build *The Gates of Heaven and Hell*. Meanwhile, Ace Jogo and Jacob prepared for battle.

"They should be here soon. Be ready because introductions won't be needed," said Ace.

"Talk to Anon. See if you can find him," said Jacob.

"I will after those idiots die," said Ace.

It became foggy; the air was still, the moon was at its peak. It was about midnight when they appeared.

"Here they are. Get ready and remember no mercy."

The fight had begun. Ace fought Roger, Jacob fought Pierre, and Jogo fought Calypso. It seemed like hours. Everyone was deep in battle; all of a sudden Jacob falls to the ground from a vital hit. He remained still on his knees when Pierre was ready to kill.

"It is time I end you," said Pierre. Jacob moves out of the way of Pierre's attack.

"You have to do better than that. Kill me fool," Jacob taunted Pierre.

Pierre screams, "Ahhh!"

The battle continued. Fatigue was set in, but no one was ready to give up. Everybody was fighting for their lives.

"No more games Calypso. Prove your loyalty to me," said Ace.

Jogo and Calypso stopped fighting for a moment.

"What did you say?" Roger shockingly asked.

Roger and Ace started talking in the midst of fighting.

"You heard me. He planned this," said Ace.

"I knew it I should've kill him," said Pierre.

The battle paused. For a moment everybody froze, time seemed to have stood still. Then Roger and Pierre both fell from a fatal strike. Ace had finished his task.

"Thank you Calypso," said Ace.

"I told you I was on your side," said Calypso.

"Could have fooled me," said Jacob.

"Me too, I almost died," said Jogo.

Then they stitched Jacob thankful to have won.

Chapter 18: Finding Anon

I finally woke up from being knocked out when Sheira appeared. "How does it feel being captured?" she asked.

"Like home," I said sarcastically.

"Hahaa… Get comfy you will be here for a while. And don't try to talk to anybody. Nobody talks to their self anymore," said Sheira. I didn't care. I was determined to talk to Ace, "Ace you hear me?"

"You don't listen do you?" she asked.

I said, "No now leave so I can talk to myself,"

"Ace we have him on Grief Mountain. Come and you may die like all the others," said Sheira.

I said, "Thanks."

"Have you heard of Grief Mountain?" asked Ace.

"I have," said Jogo. He asked, "What for?"

"That is where Anon has been taken," said Ace.

"But it's a wasteland. Why would they go there? No life exists on the mountains," said Jogo.

"It's a trap," said Jacob.

"I know, but Anon didn't contest her. It must be true," said Ace.

"Ok let's go," said Jogo.

"Wait I want to try something," said Ace.

Ace sat down and tried to *Enlighten* me again. He wanted clues to find me.

"If only I could tell him how to get here. What did she say? *I see the grief, find the path... to life and death at peace*," I was trying to remember the mythical verse.

"I just learned a new trick. I can visualize and hear anybody through *Enlightenment*," said Ace.

"Tell us what you saw and heard," said Jogo.

"I saw Anon tied up in a garden with a pool of water," said Ace.

"Did he say anything?" asked Jacob.

Ace said, "Yea, he said *I see the grief, find the path… to life and death at peace.*"

"So, there is a garden in the mountain…," said Jacob.

"And we have to find the hidden path where Grim is hiding," said Jogo.

"Takes us to the mountain Jogo," said Ace assertively.

"What about me?" asked Calypso.

"We could use another hand," said Ace.

"I'm coming too," said Calypso.

"Alright this way, we must go underground," said Jogo.

"Why?" asked Jacob.

"It is the only way. It could take a week or two. The undergrounds can be tricky.

Two days passed and they were almost there. They were no longer underground. They were in the woods. It was breezy and the sun was rising. You could hear life as it woke with the sun.

"Are we close, because I have never heard of this mountain," said Calypso.

"No one has ever returned from this mountain. Grim and his partner are the only exceptions. And Grim is also dead," said Jogo.

A few more days passed before they arrived at the base of the mountain. Jogo said, "This is as far as I can take us. The rest is up to you Ace."

Ace said, "*I see the grief, find the path… to life and death at peace.*"

A shadow casted over the mountain then the path appeared. "Aww, the magic words," said Ace.

"Finally I can breathe. Death is not my forte," said Jacob.

"Say no more, it is time to prepare ourselves for a victorious battle," said Ace.

"Yes, for G.O.D. is my only witness," said Jacob.

They worked their way through the cave to find a vibrant garden, a pool of crystal clear water, Grim, Sheira, and I. They were shocked to see Grim in human form.

Sheira introduced herself, "I am Sheira. I am queen of life goddess of war. This is my home and you aren't welcome."

"Hold on, they are the first visitors to see the cave. Don't forget Anon was our guest too," said Grim.

"Let's talk," said Ace.

"I need Anon and I need you," said Grim.

"What for?" asked Ace.

"You killed my brother, Pigeon…," said Shira.

"And ya'll are the key to the gates," said Grim.

"*The Gates of Judgment* were destroyed," said Ace.

"Only the structure was destroyed. The gates were unharmed. Also it was your blood that made it possible to pass judgment. You opened *The Gates of Judgment*," said Grim.

"What?" Ace said feeling confused.

"Your blood and my ritual," said Sheira.

"For what?" asked Ace.

"We are G.O.D. We control the fate of the world. Anon will open *The Gates of Heaven and Hell*, so we may bring back to life those that we choose," said Grim.

"Why? Only the gates pass judgment," said Ace.

"Not anymore. Fight me if you must. I'm ready. My flesh has come back, so I'm mortal again.

"So you just want to become the undisputed ruler..." implied Ace.

"With my princes and my queen," said Grim.

"I'm willing to overlook my brother's death for ultimate ruler," said Sheira.

"I don't know what to say," Ace paused before continuing, "But let's end this while we are here. And let Anon go. You have his blood."

"I want you dead now. You had your chance," said Sheira before she attacked Ace.

"Fine let's do this. Go get Anon," said Ace.

Sheira and Ace fought while Jogo and Jacob went to get me. Then Calypso decided to attack Grim.

"So you are challenging me?" said Grim.

"Of course, after what you put me through," said Calypso.

"I need to fight. They can't win fighting alone," said Anon while being carried to safety. They were fighting for a long time. No one wanted to die. Then Grim disappeared.

"Where are you Grim?" asked Calypso looking for Grim.

Grim appears and slashes him in the back. They continued fighting. Calypso slashed Grim's robe leaving him unharmed. Then Grim stabs Calypso through the heart.

"You truly are the fool," said Grim taunting Calypso as he died.

"Help me I can't fight much longer," said Sheira. Then Ace slits her throat killing her in the process.

"That is for my fallen brothers. Are you ready?" asked Ace.

"Yes, let's fight," said Grim. They exchange words as they fought.

"Are you going to kill me?" asked Grim taunting Ace.

"I thought you were a healer," said Ace.

"I am healed, so I'm back to my old reaping self," said Grim.

"I'm here," said Jacob.

Ace yelled, "No, go help Anon. This is my fight."

Ace and Grim cut each other simultaneously, but the fight goes on. It seemed like hours. Then Grim falls to his knees, weakened from his human form.

"I'm immortal; this can't be," said Grim.

"Not anymore," said Ace and he cuts Grim's head off. Ace had finished his last task, *Trap the Rat*. Life and death was, finally, at peace.

Ace went to check on me, "Are you alright Anon?"

"Yea, I'm ready to marry Na'ina too," I said jokingly.

It was over for now until death rises again.

Who is the main character?

Anon the Unknown/ the narrator

What is the point of view?

First person

Who was Grim trying to deceive?

Everybody

Does Calypso survive if he doesn't betray Pierre and Pigeon?

Opinionated question

What is the significance of Na'ina?

None other than helping Anon reach his potential.

Is this a book of religious beliefs or a book of ideas and
philosophy?

Ideas and philosophy

What type of book is this?

Compare and contrast